CW00558398

In His Lordship's House of Ill Fame

Steamy Trials of a Victorian Lady, Volume 2

Catherine Moorland

Published by northanger books, 2023.

IN HIS LORDSHIP'S HOUSE OF ILL FAME

First edition. October 5, 2023.

Copyright © 2023 Catherine Moorland.

ISBN: 979-8223462583

Written by Catherine Moorland.

Also by Catherine Moorland

Demon Lover Romance
Riding a Monster Wave at BDSM Beach

Steamy Trials of a Victorian Lady
In His Lordship's Dovecote
In His Lordship's House of Ill Fame

For Marek, who first awakened my interest in history and introduced me to the novels of Thackeray and Jane Austen.

PROLOGUE: THE STORY SO FAR

It's a week since Jonathon Gilbey, the arrogant and impossibly handsome young naturalist and follower of Darwin arrived at Henshawe Hall to conduct experiments in Sir Jeffrey Henshawe's dovecote. Over the course of those seven days Lady Emily has fought a losing battle with the passionate attraction she feels towards the youth. Her initial attempts to convert him to religion have succumbed to his noble face and fine physique. Simply commanding Jonathon to quit Henshawe Hall has merely resulted in further delicious intimacies, and when Emily slips away from the grand ball held in honour of her thirtieth birthday her resistance collapses entirely. So passionate is their love-making on the floor of her husband's dovecote Emily is convinced that she is pregnant. Jonathon flees to London. Emily immerses herself in Darwin's writings and becomes Hampshire's leading female advocate for 'survival of the fittest', but nothing can fill the gap Jonathon's absence makes in her heart. Certain that she is pregnant and that the inevitable discovery of her condition will lead to disgrace and ruin, Emily is left with only one means of concealing her scandalous affair. She and Sir Jeffrey haven't had sexual relations for many years. Still stunningly beautiful and helplessly attractive, Emily must seduce her husband anew. But in spite of her best efforts, Sir Jeffrey's disinterest in her body remains adamant, and even shows signs, not merely of disinterest, but of a settled aversion. At her wits' end, Emily learns that her husband's lack of enthusiasm for her love stems from a shocking perversion. She must lay herself open to unspeakable desires if she's to save herself from destruction.

CHAPTER ONE: THE MORNING AFTER

It was the morning after the ball, the grand ball to celebrate her thirtieth birthday. Lady Emily sat at the breakfast table with her house guests.

She was exhausted. Her body ached. She'd only slept three hours.

Her guests wouldn't stop peppering her with questions.

Lady Penrose was particularly insistent:

"But what happened to you last night, my dear?" Lady Penrose always badgered people but this morning her tone was particularly hectoring. "We were so worried about you!"

"Where did you get to, Emily?" asked pushy Mrs Smith.

"'Lor how we missed you!" probed Viscountess de Vaughan with her own particular brand of cattiness. "Slipping away from your own birthday ball! At midnight! At the height of the celebrations!"

Mister Smith beamed at her:

"Whatever could have got into you, my lady? Dashing off into the night!"

Emily parried their questions as best she could. It was fortunate that her husband seemed the least inquisitive of the whole party. She tried to invent convincing explanations, or at least pretty ones:

"... Oh... oh nothing... nothing really... I didn't 'dash off into the night'... I just needed a little fresh air, that's all... some time alone to ponder my new life... one's birthday... it's not every night a woman turns thirty..."

She wasn't a good liar. She prayed that the pallor of her complexion, the darkness around her eyes—her mirror had instantly betrayed her this morning—weren't going to betray her to her guests.

"She's hiding something!" said Viscountess de Vaughan, her certainty somewhat barbed.

"A little fresh air indeed!" cried Mrs Smith.

Emily wasn't sure how long she could withstand their pestering. She was exhausted. She hadn't got to bed till after five a.m, and she'd been woken again by her maid at eight. Her body felt limp and heavy. There was a raw ache between her legs where Mister Gilbey's magnificent manhood had hammered into her helpless surrender. She still felt a prickling warmth where his generous seed had pumped into her melting depths, a reason for even greater anxiety.

"Emily loves her fresh air," said Sir Jeffrey. Her husband's complacency, usually so galling, felt like a kindness this morning. He was a good man really. "A midnight stroll in the park, it's just the sort of quirk gets into my lady's pretty little head."

The way he said 'pretty' and 'little' didn't irritate her the way they usually did.

Her shoulders were still uncomfortably abraded where Jonathan had pounded her into the cobble stone floor of the dovecote. It was fortunate the dress she was wearing this morning buttoned up high and swept low around her ankles concealing the bruises her hips had suffered and the teeth marks on her breasts. There wasn't an inch of her that Jonathon hadn't printed himself upon.

"She missed the highlight of the evening!" protested the vicar. "La Valse Grande de Monsieur Strauss!"

She'd fucked her husband's ornithological expert on the floor of the dovecote. As weary as she was, the thought sent a wild thrill surging through her body. She and Mister Gilbey. They'd fucked. Rutted. They'd swythed on cobblestones sticky with pigeon droppings, a pair of wild animals writhing on the jungle floor, or angels copulating on the pavements of paradise, she didn't know which.

She had too many things to worry about to be able to really think clearly. Jonathon was gone. Mister Gilbey had caught the first train back to London. He'd given her the address of the hotel where he'd be staying, begged her to send him a letter... but what would she write? *That she was pregnant?* She wouldn't know for sure for another month... the dazed fulfillment ticking inside her might just be the after-effect of her disordered night... but she knew... she already knew... a change had come over her last night... such ecstasy—and such dread— don't strike one without being stricken utterly... she could wait for doctors and more obvious bodily evidence but in her heart Emily knew she was already with child.

"I didn't see Gilbey at last nights festivities, my lord," said the vicar.

"No. 'Fraid not." How amiable her husband's oblivious absorption in his pigeons seemed this morning! "He had to return to London on the spur of the moment, what?"

Sir Jeffrey was a good man in his way. He was kind and considerate. He'd always treated her with the greatest respect. It was natural that an educated man should be interested in science, even to the exclusion of all else. It wasn't his fault that their marital congress had never amounted to much or that intercourse had petered out more than five years ago. *Five years!* If she was pregnant her life was finished.

"Quite the barn storming Darwinian, our Mister Gilbey!"

The vicar was still smarting from the blows Jonathon had dealt him in debate.

"Survival of the fittest, what?" said Mister Smith.

Lord Penrose chuckled.

"Nature red in tooth and claw!"

"Yes," explained her husband. "Gilbey's Darwin's number one acolyte. They say the young fellow's Mister Darwin's right-hand man. He's sailing with our eminent naturalist on this new expedition of his."

Her heart froze. Cold sweat beaded her forehead. An expedition? Jonathon hadn't mentioned an expedition. Her voice quavered:

"An expedition, my lord?"

"One of your full-blown, scientific, expeditionary voyages!" chuckled her husband. "Galapagos Islands! Tierra del Fuego! That sort of thing. Picking up fossils and the sea gull's latest mutations." Everyone laughed. "Gilbey's joining the expedition. That's why he had to get back to London post haste."

Surely not!

The Galapagos Islands? Mister Darwin's last Galapagos Islands expedition had taken nearly five years!

It couldn't be! Jonathon loved her. She and Jonathon were in love. They'd sealed their love last night on the floor of the dovecote! He'd only hurried back to London because staying at Henshawe Hall without declaring his love to the world was too painful.

Mrs Smith's eyes filled with worry.

"Are you alright, Lady Emily?"

Concerned faces pressed in around her.

"... Yes... yes... I'm fine, thank you... I'm... perfectly fine..."

It was only a matter of time before the concerned expressions turned to hard-eyed interrogations, probing for her secret.

Her secret was already out, or would be out by the end of the day, unless her maid proved reliable.

It had been five a.m, the East just beginning to grow light, when she'd slipped back into her bedroom, fairly sure that no one had seen her leave the dovecote. Three hours of troubled sleep had been disturbed by a knock at the door. Just the usual eight o'clock knock. Mary with hot water for her bath.

God, how she'd needed that bath! She'd cleaned herself up as best she could at the dovecote tap, but she'd still felt sticky all over, and there was her gown, the magnificent, voluminous, revealing blue satin, smeared with bird droppings.

"I fear the water's a little too hot, my lady. Perhaps you should wait a minute."

"... No... no... it's not too hot at all..."

She'd worn a cotton slip in the bath, the usual cotton slip she wore when she bathed. It covered the worst of the bites and bruises but there were still some teeth marks on her shoulders, even round her throat, that could only signify one thing.

Mary had seen alright. Mary had noticed immediately. Mary's chirpy questions about the ball had instantly turned to oblique inquiries as to when my lady got in.

"... Oh... around two I think... I'm not quite sure... yes, around two o'clock I think it was..."

"Do you want me to get this washed?"

Mary was holding the gown! She'd dug it out from under the bed where Emily had thrust it when she got in. The swags of blue satin stunk.

"... Yes... please... if you don't mind..."

"I don't mind, my lady. I'll do it meself, so's laundry don't go getting no ideas."

Mary knew. She was an intelligent young woman. Mary no doubt knew more about the ways of love than 'my lady' did. Her maid had always been trustworthy up till now. But up till now there'd never been a secret she'd needed to charge her maid to keep.

Perhaps a bribe would be in place. Maybe she could offer Mary money to hold her tongue...

... She'd blushed with shame...

... A sense of disgrace had flooded over her...

... Offer Mary money...?

... It was tantamount to corrupting her maid. A bribe was no better than enticing a servant to sin. Mary was a good-natured girl. She might not even accept a bribe!

... She could dismiss her, invent some crime that the maid had committed and send her packing...

... No...

... Never...

... Out of the question...

She'd fornicated with a stranger. She'd committed adultery, but she wasn't yet so deeply dyed in sin that she could injure an innocent girl.

How could she even have thought of such a thing? Does being an animal in heat rutting on the jungle floor put these terrible things into your mind?

... Does rutting on the jungle floor put even more abominable ideas into your brain...?

... If she was pregnant *she was going to need some way of convincing Sir Jeffrey that the child was his*...

... And there was only one way she could possibly do that, *and that route was barred to her*... that means of deceiving her husband was an utter impossibility...

... She and Sir Jeffrey hadn't had sexual intercourse for nearly five years. There was no possibility of resuming their relations now. Sir Jeffrey's disinterest in physical love was absolute. She remembered the fury with which he'd greeted her attempt to sleep with him, less than a week ago. She couldn't help recalling the hint of menace in his smile, the dark distaste, almost lustful in itself, with which he'd thrust her away from him when, fearful of the moral peril she was in, she'd attempted to seduce him. Not even the family name or the Henshawe lineage disturbed his disinterest in her body. Sir Jeffrey cared not a whit that the estate would have no heir. He'd already entailed Henshawe Hall to the son of a second cousin. Sir Jeffrey was a good kind man at heart. The discovery that a bastard had been fathered on his wife would kill him.

The breakfast table crowded in on her.

"Are you alright, my dear? You look quite pale."

There was too much to do, too many things to decide, every single choice confronting her unthinkable.

"The excitement of the ball must have taken it out of her!" remarked Lady Penrose.

Emily's head did in fact spin. Write to Jonathon? Speak to Mary? Face her husband's wrath? There were so many things to confront she didn't know where to start.

"She's had a long night," said the Viscountess.

"... Yes... yes..." said Emily... "... I have... a long night... I believe I'll just... I'll just go and have a lie down for a minute if I may..."

CHAPTER TWO: JONATHON'S LETTER

Emily put off writing to Jonathon all that afternoon.

How could she write to her lover—was that even what he was?—before she knew for certain whether she was with child or not?

Surely Jonathon wasn't going on Mister Darwin's expedition! He couldn't be away for five years. Her need to know grew desperate, but taking pen in hand was beyond her.

Mary. First she needed to sort out where she stood with her maid.

They were alone in her bedroom at last. Emily faltered:

"... Did you manage to wash my gown, Mary...?"

"Yes, ma-am. I did."

Mary was brushing her hair preparatory to getting dressed for dinner. Eight o'clock and she still hadn't written to Jonathon!

"... Did the... erm... stains come out...?"

"Not quite, ma-am. Some were quite obdurate."

Obdurate? Emily had a feeling her maid had chosen the word especially.

"What do you think the stain could have been? I don't think I brushed against anything nasty. I've no idea."

"Bird poop, begging your ladyship's pardon. Perhaps your ladyship ventured into the dovecote?"

Ventured? 'Ventured' too had a risqué ring to it.

"... Yes... perchance I did... I can't remember..."

The tug and rustle of the brush in her hair grew soothing. Mary brushed thoughtfully, combing the luster back into Emily's raven black hair in the mirror.

"'Tis a dangerous place for a ball gown— the dovecote— my lady. Especially blue satin."

She knew. Mary knew everything. Only twenty-one, but Mary was already far more experienced than she. Mary'd already had a number of liaisons with various members of staff. She even had a child, by the footman, living with her mother. Mary saw the whole situation. She was plaiting the braids that looked so well in the lustrous torrent of Emily's mane in a thoughtful manner.

Emily drew a deep breath.

"... Can I trust you, Mary...?"

She'd always got on well with her maid, but this sudden dread was appalling, committing herself to an intimacy that went beyond all bounds.

"... Can I trust you not to tell Sir Jeffrey...?"

"Sir Jeffrey? Lor, why should I tell Sir Jeffrey, maam?"

"... Or... or anyone else...?"

Her maid had a melodiously natural laugh.

"What business is it of anyone else but you, my lady? Sure, we gals need a few secrets of our own. There's matters we like to keep to ourselves."

'Gals?' Mary would never have dared call her a 'gal' a week ago.

"... Well then... good... thank you..."

****

She escaped from the dinner table around eleven and finally got down to writing her letter.

Dear ~~Mister~~, ~~Jonathon~~, ~~Mister Gilbey~~, *sir,*

I miss you terribly—it was true, she might as well write it— *the events of last night have quite o'er-topped me. I trust you are well and arrived in London safely*—so smug and noncommittal!— *I long to see you again,* ~~to look into your eyes and feel your arms around me, and to~~—what if the letter's opened, her missive spied upon?— *I hear that Mister Darwin is to organize another expedition. Five years? Please tell me that it isn't true. I beg you to ensure me that I am not to endure a protracted suffering.*

Your absence, even for these last few lonely hours, has been more than I can bear—oh God! What is she saying? 'Suffering?' Last night was the high point of her existence, her life's supreme ecstasy— *I fear*—how should she put this? How can she write this down? Even for Mary's eyes?— *that our genes may have made their natural selection, in fact I'm already quite sure of it, even though it's so early and...* she bit the end of her pen... *if that be so I know not what to do in regards to my husband*—so cold! So calculating! Her heart on fire, her body in Hell flames already and she writes like a pernickety spinster!—*I love you. I always will.* ~~Yours sincerely,~~ ~~Lady~~... *Your loving Ape...*

She sealed the letter and gave it to Mary.

"First thing! Tomorrow, Mary! The village post office, if you will!"

She dared not commit her missive to the daily postal collection from the Hall.

****

A week later she received a reply.

Mister Gilbey's letter both enraptured and appalled her.

He was in love with her. Jonathon loved her to the bottom of his soul. She was the only woman in his life. She'd redeemed him and given new meaning to his days. Her heart expanded in joy and pride as she read....

... He'd also, he explained, dedicated his life to science. He'd committed himself body and soul to the pursuit of empirical evidence and experimental truth. He had a second mistress besides his 'loving Ape' and that mistress was the Theory of Evolution. He'd miss her. It would be painful beyond endurance to be separated from her by the best part of the longitude of the globe but yes, he was to embark with Mister Darwin on the forthcoming expedition to the Galapagos Islands. He hoped she understood. He'd only be gone five years...

Five years?

If she was pregnant their baby would be born by then! Jonathon hadn't even bothered to reply concerning her fear—the certainty in her heart—that she was already carrying his child!

If she was in fact pregnant their child would be over *four years old* by the time he got back! And she'd be living in penury and disgrace the minute her husband discovered that her 'offspring' wasn't his!

Jonathon's professions of love were all very well, but the purport of his letter was so cold and businesslike!

There was even a list of demands, practical demands, that he begged to make of her.

As well as professing his 'undying love' Jonathon's letter asked her to forward some books and papers he'd left behind in his 'precipitous flight from the lodestone of his love', with an address in London where he could be reached if she wished to 'come to him and renew their union.'

Her blood boiled. Her head spun. Slip away to the metropolis so he could fuck her again? Rush up to London to be plunged in ruin even deeper than she was plunged in ruin already? Did Mister Gilbey not realize that it was mid summer? That good society *fled* the heat and squalor of London in June, and that she wouldn't have a chance to see him again in the metropolis till the winter season came? He'd probably be halfway down the damned Atlantic by then!

"You're looking a little peaked this morning, my dear," said her husband over the breakfast table.

She blanched. A mere week had passed since the night in the dovecote. Surely it couldn't be morning sickness so soon!

Lord Penrose guffawed:

"Got out of bed on the wrong side, what?" Lord Penrose had a particularly irritating laugh. He sounded like a donkey braying. "You need to take her down to Weymouth, Jeffrey. Get some sea air in those pretty lungs!"

Lord Penrose thought himself funny. He was always laughing at his own jokes. He ogled her 'pretty lungs!'

"Mister Smith takes me down to Weymouth every August for my emphysema!" chirruped Mrs Smith. "We have our own bathing machine!"

"We certainly do!" assented Mister Smith.

That was another failing of Sir Jeffrey's. Another thing about her husband that she couldn't stand.

Guests!

The house was always full of guests!

It was full of guests again this morning! A mere week after their grand ball and Henshawe Hall was packed again! Her husband couldn't stop inviting people! Shooting parties and boating parties and dinner parties that lasted a week. Sir Jeffrey loved a crowded breakfast table. He did it so he'd never have to spend any time alone with her.

"I prefer Biarritz to Weymouth," said Viscountess de Vaughan, a hint of venom in her archness.

"Biarritz?" cried Lord Penrose. "Full of confounded frogs!"

He laughed uproariously. The man was an utter bore. God knows how Lady Penrose put up with him.

Her husband smiled at her, his usual anxious, caring, blandly unseeing smile.

"I'll take you to Biarritz if it will raise your spirits, my lady."

Her husband was a nice man, really. Far nicer than Lord Penrose. Far handsomer too.

With his thrusting upper lip and snarling smile, Lord Penrose was a complete fright.

Emily studied her husband's face. She often forgot how good looking Sir Jeffrey was for a man of thirty five, his face a little immobile for her taste, but immobile with good breeding and a certain distinction. He was certainly well built too.

Her husband was much more nobly built than Lord Penrose with his fat belly and bulging chest and splayed legs at the breakfast table.

It was no surprise really that her husband was well built. He rode to hounds. He practiced fencing. Her husband was a capable swordsman. He even did construction work improving his dovecote. When he leaned back in a chair he crossed his legs with due decorum, but they were nice enough legs in their way. The more she thought about it the more Emily realized that her husband could even be said to be a 'catch.' She'd certainly fancied him once, many years ago...

... She needed to fancy him now...

... Just a single night's love was all she required to free herself from this fear that, if she was indeed pregnant—and in her heart she knew she was— the author of her condition would remain concealed and Sir Jeffrey wouldn't cast her out.

She smiled:

"... Yes... perhaps... Biarritz... Biarritz might be just the thing for me...!"

Yes. Her mind was made up. She refused to be ruined. There was no time to wait for doctors and bodily evidence. She daren't risk putting it off till her condition was proven and her fate sealed. There was only one thing she could do. She wouldn't let them cast her and Jonathon's child down into penury and disgrace. Morality? Morality didn't come into it. It was survival of the fittest. Beast eat beast in the primal jungle. She'd have sexual intercourse with Sir Jeffrey come Hell nor high water. She'd lie with her husband and make him believe that the child she was all but certain she was carrying was his. She had no other option. Yes. She'd fuck Sir Jeffrey if it was the last thing she did... he was already looking a little more attractive.

CHAPTER THREE: WILD ATTEMPTS

It was all very well making decisions about seduction, telling herself she'd rut with her husband come Hell nor high water. Achieving that end proved to be another matter entirely.

She was too hesitant. Too clumsy. Too obvious.

Her attempts at seduction proved unsuccessful.

Sir Jeffrey's disinterest in sexual intercourse ran deeper than disinterest normally runs. It felt more, in fact, like an aversion.

Emily knew how irresistible she could be, how voluptuous her body could feel with a man who truly desired her. Sir Jeffrey didn't desire her. He made that much obvious. It was almost as if he felt a physical loathing for the wife he cherished in every other way. Whatever she did to allure him—she hadn't needed to even try to be alluring with Jonathon— her husband's resistance only grew more adamant. She tried to remember the girlish tricks she'd used to arouse his lust when they were first married—those poor comings-together that had never produced an heir to Henshawe Hall—but it was all too long ago.

She cornered him alone in the dovecote—surely an exciting place for him as much as for her—and let him know with the deftest of touches and closest skimming of lips that she was there to be taken. He clambered up a ladder to inspect a recent hatching.

She pretended one night to have drunk too much wine and sneaked into his bed. He'd turned his back on her.

Even her finest stratagem failed. Jonathon's delicious scratches and luscious love-bites now vanished, her bath tub filled with steaming water, her bathing robe adhering to her still shapely body, wet cotton showing off her engorged nipples and clinging to her winged hips, she'd faked a sudden illness, a passing seizure, got Mary to summon her husband, begged the maid to leave her alone with her husband while the seizure passed and her hot need rose from the steam and water into Sir Jeffrey's arms, her shapely breasts wetting the front of his shirt, her succulent surrender searching for his weapon through his trousers, now was surely the moment for him to possess her and for the dreadful situation she was in to be resolved.

Nothing.

Not a quiver.

Not a tingle of awakened desire.

Just awkwardness and embarrassment on both sides.

Only a bland but firm caringness on her husband's side, forgiveness for her temporary 'disorder', the doctor summoned and a dreadful interview with the medic during which she feared she would be found out.

The days ticked by. Her chances of deceiving Sir Jeffrey grew fewer and fewer. A week had already passed since Jonathon possessed her on the dovecote floor and, fully convinced she was pregnant, she still hadn't found a means of passing her baby off as her husband's.

It was hopeless. Her life was over. Her days at Henshawe Hall were numbered. She could flee to London, into Jonathon's arms, but his letters explained how busy he was giving lectures on Evolution at the Royal Geographical Society and preparing for his Galapagos expedition. She was welcome to come to London if it was to 'renew their union' but more substantial support was clearly not on offer. His letters didn't even comment on her conviction that she was with child.

Emily brooded bitterly on the merciless blows of fate and the heedless nature of men. She grew grimly self-absorbed. Her broodings led her down hidden pathways deep inside her she'd never even realized were waiting to waylay her.

It was now a whole three weeks since her rut on the dovecote floor, wild fears and fantastic certainties swirling more and more violently in her head, and still no hope in sight.

Sitting at her window watching the gloom of another summer's evening take hold of the dark cypresses at the end of the fading garden, there was a knock at the door.

She didn't raise her head. Emily wished fervently to be left alone.

The door opened and Mary came in. Her maid's voice had grown subdued and anxious of late:

"Are you alright, my lady? You keep to your room so!"

"… Yes.. yes… fine… I'm fine, Mary… please… leave me to myself…"

"I cannot, maam. I can't bear to see you like this." Mary *pitied* her! "To watch what's going on!"

Emily couldn't refrain from a bitter cry:

"And what's that, Mary?"

Mary knew everything. Mary knew all her secret fears and hopes, her forlorn longing for Mister Gilbey, her pathetic attempts on Sir Jeffrey, but not even the most confidential of maid servants could understand the sorrow racking her heart.

"You're fear that you're…"

"Not fear, Mary! Certainty!"

"Hush, maam. 'Tis too soon. Us women can jump to conclusions too easily. You don't know for sure. It could be just nerves, my lady."

The slip of a girl was lecturing her! Mary was accusing her of hysteria! She cried out:

"The heart knows things beyond the grasp of doctors and foolish maids!"

"Yes. I know, maam, but… difficulties with your husband…"

She ought to send Mary away. She was the wife of a nobleman. It was wrong to be discussing her marital difficulties with a servant. Every way she looked, she was in the wrong. Emily sighed bitterly:

"My husband!"

She heard the bustle of Mary's skirt, the warmth of the girl sitting close beside her.

"Your husband, maam…"

"He's a stone! A block of wood! Dead to me! Not one stirring of regard!"

She felt Mary's hand settled gently on her heaving shoulder. Her maid was patting her on the shoulder! She was being comforted by a servant! It was unthinkable!

"Don't say that, milady. If you really believe you're pregnant... perchance there's a way of convincing Sir Jeffrey the babe's his own."

"Oh yes! Right! Wonderful! When I'm married to a stone! A block of wood!"

Mary knew enough about her failed seductions to realize the hopelessness of her situation.

"Not quite, ma-am. Not quite a stone. Lord Jeffrey isn't quite a block of wood when it comes to..."

"Sex! Fornication! *Fucking!* Call it by its name!"

Mary murmured.

"Then... fucking, maam... when it comes to fucking... some men are just made different from others... that's all..."

Twenty-year-old Mary honouring her with her with her wealth of experience! It was intolerable!

"*That's all?* Made different?! *Made to punish helpless women!*"

"... No, maam, no... you mustn't say it..." Mary drew in a deep breath. "... I don't believe Sir Jeffrey's completely cold, not when it comes to fucking... in fact..."

Good God! Her husband was doing it with Mary! He couldn't manage with his wife but a slutty servant could get his juices flowing!

Mary laughed.

"... No... no, my lady. Nothing like that. Nothing like that at all... you see..." She paused. She looked into Emily's eyes. "... There's an establishment in Winchester..."

"Establishment?"

The word jolted her.

Parliament was an establishment. Her husband represented the county. The Church of England was an establishment. They went to St John's every Sunday. What did Mary mean, an 'establishment?'

"... Well... house, my lady... a house where men go to... you know... satisfy themselves in whichever way appeals..."

"Appeals?"

"... To their lower natures, maam... you see, Sir Jeffrey..."

Emily was suddenly stunned by her own innocence. Even possibly carrying a bastard child, she was amazed at her own incredulity. Twenty years old, and Mary knew more about the ways of the world than she did! Than she ever would!

Her husband was a 'whacking cove!'

Sir Jeffrey was a 'whipping steamer!'

He enjoyed lashing 'gals' with his riding crop, as if they were stubborn mares refusing to jump a hedge! He favored 'laying the cat on hot and hard!'

Her husband was a sadist. He relished beating prostitutes.

He paid women—often quite beautiful women according to Mary—to let him 'tan the living daylights out of them!'

"The living daylights?"

"Yes, maam. I'm told Sir Jeffrey can be quite the fierce one."

She was aghast. She was floundering in dark water, out of her depth.

"... And after he's... tanned the living daylights out of them...?"

"Oh yes, maam. Word is Sir Jeffrey rides his strumpets hard. It's said Sir Jeffrey gives cock alley a prodigious piping.'"

Emily felt ill.

Below, the park was growing dim. The cypresses swooned. Rooks cawed in the gathering darkness.

She didn't want to hear another word. Jeffrey? Her bland, preoccupied, disinterested lord and master? Attending an 'establishment'? A sadist? A follower of the Divine Marquis?

"You mean...?"

"Oh yes, maam. There's a number of Sir Jeffrey's doxies have whelped. Your husband's a good many by-blows around the county."

Emily was aghast. Terrible facts jolted into place like cogs in a disjointed machine.

There *was* rather a large amount of the estate's income going out to various 'charities' around Hampshire. Sir Jeffrey at least looked after his ill-gotten offspring.

"But..."

Her shame was complete. Her humiliation was absolute. Her husband lusted after 'doxies' but never even looked at her.

"No, maam." Mary stroked her hair. Her maid produced a handkerchief. "Don't cry. I believe—and, by my understanding of men I swear I'm right—that Sir Jeffrey is afraid of making love to you."

"Afraid?"

"He fears it, ma-am. He dreads the very thought. He's only cold and stand-offish because he's afraid that if he softens towards you even just a little, if he embarks on even the most halting of intimacies his terrible proclivity might take over, he might lose control, and because you're his wife and he loves you he might unleash his most violent punishments upon you."

Emily considered.

What Mary said could be true. Her maid might certainly be right. Sir Jeffrey did love her. He was the most solicitous of husbands, and if he was tortured by unspeakable longings...

Emily wiped her eyes. She controlled the sobs shaking her body.

"... So... so what can I do, Mary..?"

"Well..." Mary's eyes brightened. "... I happen to have a friend, maam, who knows the good lady who runs that very establishment..."

CHAPTER FOUR: THE ESTABLISHMENT IN WINCHESTER

It was an ill-looking house in a back street behind the cathedral. It was apparant that sadists liked to unleash their demons behind a blackened door down a darkened alleyway.

Inside however, behind the blackened door, the rooms were quite palatial, the furniture of the best quality. Only aristocrats and the wealthy were allowed to enter this place of sin.

The madame was a roly poly woman in a revealing gown, her smile too brazen and cheery for her to have ever felt the cat laid on hot and hard.

She looked Emily up and down. She peered hard into the black veil covering Emily's face. The finest Spanish gauze kept the woman's beady eyes out.

"Well, my dear. You certainly have the embonpoint my gentlemen favour..." Her eager eyes went down to Emily's breasts. Emily felt sick. Sir Jeffrey was one of Madam's 'gentlemen.' "... Let's have a look at your face then."

Emily stopped breathing.

"No, ma-am. My face is my own. My friend tells me..." She nodded at Mary. "... That your... staff... can go masked if they wish. It's what I wish."

"... Oh... very well..."

The woman made no attempt to hide her disappointment, but Emily's 'embonpoint' absorbed her interest too eagerly for her to demur.

"Mm. Very well. Stand up then..." Emily stood up. "... Turn around.."

Emily spun, not too coquettish-ly she hoped. The gaudy skirt, a cheap Manchester print of a Regency flamboyance, swished round her ankles.

The woman tilted her head to one side.

"Where did you say you were from?"

Emily did her best to disguise her educated accent.

"... London, maam... Bethnal Green... I've just come down... my friend tells me there's some fine thrashing coves in Winchester..."

Her voice came out silly and stupid-sounding. It was fortunate Madame was more interested in her body than her stiff upper lip.

Emily had already taken off the few rings she usually wore, her wedding ring of course, the diamond Jeffrey had given her for her twenty-fifth birthday. Mary had advised her that it was imperative she present herself as a working class dollymop. The establishment had strict rules against upper class women slumming it. If a customer chanced to whip his strumpet too vigorously, Madame dare not risk the strumpet's having blue blood and taking her wounds to the police.

The woman remarked:

"You talk rather nice for Bethnal Green, lass. You sure you can take your licking when a gentleman puts his back into it?"

"Sure I can. I've worked the Garden, maam. My flashman was a terror with the birch."

Emily couldn't help her educated enunciation but at least Mary had coached her in the language of the gutter. In fact the vile words were rolling effortlessly from her pampered lips.

"And afters? When the gentlemen want their afters?"

"Cock alley's always open for afters, maam."

Her replies seemed to satisfy Madame.

"Very well then, missy."

It seemed that Emily was accepted as a scion of the establishment.

A name was chosen for her— 'Posy'— it felt like a rather shrinking violet sort of name for a buttered bun strumpet but the lady of the house was a Romantic.

There was some debate about terms.

The house charged its gentlemen an entrance fee of two guineas.

Two guineas seemed about right for enduring a night's pain. However it turned out that eighty percent of the entrance fee went to the establishment. Only five shillings and thruppence went to the girl who was to be whipped. Anything over and above five shillings and thruppence depended on the sadists' generosity.

"Don't worry, my dear. A figure like yours, I'm sure you'll get some big tips."

Emily had a jewelry box at home with thousands of pounds worth of gold, diamonds, sapphires and emeralds in it. Big tips were neither here nor there. Of greater concern was her starting time.

Madame looked at her watch. It was four o'clock, a Tuesday afternoon.

"You can rest up here till we open."

The woman was all for Emily starting work on the spot, in fact tonight, and for Emily to work every single night for at least the first month. She'd be a broken-down whipping horse before her husband even showed his face at the establishment.

"Tonight, dearie. No toe in the water. Best jump straight in."

Madame's roving eye made it clear that, having satisfied herself as to the voluptuous curves under Emily's Manchester print, she was as anxious to get a look at Emily's naked body as any whipping steamer could be.

"... No... Friday..." said Emily. "... Please... being new to Winchester, maam, I've a few things need sorting out first... this Friday... I promise faithfully..."

The woman scowled.

"Very well then. Friday."

"At...?"

"Eleven," said Madame huffily. "We keep society hours."

Emily smiled.

"I'll see you at eleven then. Friday night at eleven."

Friday was Sir Jeffrey's Winchester day. Her husband came into town every Friday to settle the parliamentary business he had in the county seat. The parliamentary business always kept him till late in the evening, obliging him to sleep in town and come back to Henshawe Hall the following morning.

****

The next Friday, dawn broke clear and sunny. By eight o'clock the temperature was already getting up. They were in for a hot day.

After lunch Sir Jeffrey gave her his usual peck on the cheek and gathered up an armful of papers from his study and stepped into Henshawe Hall's manorial landau. When he went to Winchester on business her husband always took the grandest of their conveyances, the roof drawn down to protect him from the sun, the estate's best horses chafing at the bit.

"I'll see you tomorrow, my dear. I should be back for lunch."

At eight that evening, immediately after dinner, Emily slipped out of the house, hurried past the dovecote where she'd sealed her fate, and crept into the coach house.

She hadn't been sure what to wear.

Mary said that the establishment provided their 'slaves'—the word set off a frisson of dread— with appropriate uniforms— Emily shuddered at the thought—so she'd chosen a simple white cotton dress, the sort of dress an unmarried country girl might wear to church in order to show off her innocence to the congregation and catch herself a husband.

She'd also brought her own mask— God knows what sort of facial coverings Madame might provide—a paste-and-feather, myriad-hued bird of paradise mask with a golden beak. She tried it on. The paste and diamanté did something magical to her cheek-bones. The gold beak housed her retroussé nose quite ominously. Multi-colored feathers fanned out from her forehead like a swathe of phosphorescent jungle blades. The mask didn't cover her mouth, but the effect was so startling that not even Jeffrey would recognize the moist cupid's-bow of her lips. God knows he'd kissed them seldom enough.

The mask was well made, with a sturdy buckle. At least, when it came time to put it on, she'd be sure no rough hand could snatch her facial covering off, not until it was time to reveal herself to Sir Jeffrey.

The brougham stood waiting, Mary already seated in the poky, but enclosed box, a lad Mary had requisitioned from the village mounted outside, in charge of the single horse.

"Well then!" said Emily. "... Here we are...!" Her heart fluttered its frantic wings in her chest. She cried up through the window. "... Drive on, my good man!"

****

It was a little after ten when their brougham rolled into the dimly lit streets of Winchester. Only in the environs of the great cathedral, where the cobblestones shone beneath gas lamps, was the darkness relieved by any sign of municipal brightness.

The brougham rolled to a halt in the fetid dimness of the alleyway. The horse stamped its hooves, dropped its dung in the gutter, nervous of the shadows.

Quarter past ten.

Forty five minutes till Emily was 'on duty' as Madame put it, enrolled in the order of 'the Daughters of the Whip.'

She shivered.

Mary murmured:

"We can always go home, my lady. If you think it will be too much for you."

Her maid was right. Yes. Better to leave Winchester at once. Flee post haste back to Henshawe Hall.

Till the arrival of Mister Gilbey her life had been an idyll, a bored idyll it's true, but too delicate and refined an existence to be exchanged for the brutal goings on behind that low, dark, lowering doorway opposite...

... Except...

... If she was indeed pregnant by Jonathon— she was certain she was pregnant by Jonathon— then, in a month, two months at the most, her husband would discover her infidelity, her adultery would be announced to the world with the most blatant proofs. She'd be lost, disgraced, cast out into shame and penury forever.

"No, Mary. No. We've come this far. It's wavering now that disgraces me."

Half past ten.

They sat and waited.

The inn where Sir Jeffrey stayed when he was in Winchester stood at the further end of the lane.

At last the great cathedral clock chimed eleven.

On the first stroke of the clock—her husband was eager for his pleasures—the familiar figure, his hat drawn down over his face, slipped from the stable entrance of the inn and hurried along the footpath towards the black door.

Her heart ached. Sir Jeffrey Henshawe! Her own husband! A nobleman of unbounded refinement! At the hunt, in the dovecote, at the table, at a ball, his carriage invariably dignified. The scampering urgency of his gait horrified her. The hunger in his every step was appalling. His scurrying speed less a need to stay incognito than to get to the savage satisfaction of his desires.

He knocked on the door.

The door opened.

Her husband passed in and the door closed swiftly behind him.

A sudden conjecture took her breath away.

"He'll choose some other girl!"

Madame had a staff of at least a dozen whores. In the forty-five minutes they'd been sitting here in the brougham Emily had already seen a number of girls and seven or eight men knock at the door and be let in. "I don't want to do it with a stranger!"

Mary laughed, a little nervously.

"Don't worry, maam. You're tonight's 'new girl.'"

"New?"

"Men are all the same, my lady. They all want the establishment's latest flower."

"*All?* All of them?"

"Yes. All." Mary chuckled. "But don't worry, maam. 'Tis a refined establishment. Precedence is always given to Madame's noblest customers. As the foremost man in Hampshire, Sir Jeffrey will have precedence."

"Precedence? Are you sure?"

"Quite sure, maam."

A fresh shock assailed her. She gasped:

"Madame *knows that Sir Jeffrey is master of Henshawe Hall?*"

It seemed a perilous knowledge to entrust to a bawdy house mistress.

"Madame's discreet, my lady. She's the only one who knows who's who. The men go masked as well as the gals."

"Masked?"

Mary shrugged.

"Of course, maam. Torturers don't want their victims recognizing them. Sadists don't like their faces to be seen. It could lead to consequences. Madame's the only one who knows." Mary pouted. She nodded at Emily. "Madame'll make sure it's Sir Jeffrey who gets the new girl. Your husband will demand it, maam. The other girls are so jaded and broken-down, and the coarsest brutes to boot!"

Emily felt sick to her stomach. Her husband had precedence in the bestial masques of Hell!

She took a deep breath and put her mask on. She made sure she fastened it tight.

"Well then. If I'm to be jaded and broken down, 'tis best it's at my husband's hands."

CHAPTER FIVE: IN THE HOUSE OF THE DIVINE MARQUIS

It was dark out in the alley.

They slipped across the street without being seen.

Mary knocked at the tradesmen's entrance and they were let in. It was the first time in her life Emily had passed through a tradesmen's entrance. Dear God, let it be the last.

Madame scowled: "You're late!"

The other girls were already out in the opulent reception room entertaining the men.

Emily hurried to get changed.

"Help me, Mary. Lace me up."

"With pleasure, my lady."

"What?"

"For pleasure!"

Pantaloons?

A pair of red, baggy silk pantaloons?

The bright red silk embroidered with pagodas and willow trees and celestial musicians playing impossible instruments?

The finest silk, tight round the ankles and ballooning out around the knees and thighs like houris wear in Turkish hareems?

She slipped them on.

The smooth silk clung to her calves, embraced her knees. Ornately stitched pagodas and willow trees and celestial musicians rustled up her thighs...

... And parted between her legs...!

... Parted like the Red Sea parted for Moses...

... Leaving her sex uncovered...!

... And kept on parting behind, her bottom completely naked...

"Ey?"

Emily glanced in the mirror. She turned and looked at her backside in the mirror. A shocked bird of paradise stared down at two full moons straining in a sheen of crimson cloud.

Mary chuckled.

"The gents require speedy access to the places that matter most, maam. The whip insists on bare flesh, and yours is magnificent, my lady."

Emily quivered— with fear or indignation she couldn't tell which. She didn't feel magnificent.

"What's this?"

"Breathe in!"

Perhaps when it came time to suckle the Sultan hareem ladies bound their breasts.

Ribbons of finest scarlet silk wound under and above her breasts, bound her belly in a cat's-cradle of crimson cords and dug in hard as Mary knotted them at the back.

"Ow!"

Her maid had never laced her up so tight before.

"Ow! maam?" Mary was in high spirits. "It's hardly 'Ow!' Time yet!"

Emily fastened her mask a notch tighter. She was suddenly afraid.

"Come," said Madame. "The gentlemen are waiting."

****

In the opulent reception room at least a dozen men were at various stages of depraved fore-play with their pantaloon-d houris, her husband among them, lounging on a divan, having his champagne topped up by red-nailed fingers.

The gentlemen's masks appalled her.

Ape masks couldn't have been more horrid.

Big burly men and small lean ones— every mask was the same, a snout of black leather embossed like a dandy's riding boots.

Sink holes for the eyes and perilous slits for the mouths. Nothing to see of their faces but Emily could feel them all grinning at her.

They lounged on divans and sprawled on couches, masked girls in pantaloons matching her own perched on a knee, snuggling under an arm, offering up licentious kisses.

She glanced around in a daze.

Her husband came to a place like this? It was horrid. Unthinkable. Big bulking male bodies taking their ease with their strumpets, all of the men in regulation tie and tails, the same tie and tales Sir Jeffrey always wore when he was away on business, their eye slits filled with murky lust, their leather snouts being refreshed with gin and champagne or swooping for a proffered breast.

Mary was right about jaded and broken down. All the girls wore trophies of previous beatings on their naked bottoms, the silken ribbons bound breasts that had been subjected to savage hungers. Their various masks—fauns, elves, dryads, not uniform masks like the men's— failed to conceal the women's own hard-eyed brutishness.

It was no wonder the ape eyes in the men's sink holes fastened on her. It was no surprise the lips inside the leather snouts moistened grimly. Compared to these ravaged jades she was a tasty morsel. Her bottom was smooth and untried, her breasts still toned and shapely. She was a delicious tidbit for these bestial palates.

Emily quailed. She turned her eyes away from the 'slaves' wanton lasciviousness. Was she to end up like these women?

No. Never. Impossible. One night would be her lot. One night, and one night only. Once she'd deceived her husband, the instant she'd taken even a single seed of his lust into her body, she'd reveal herself, show him her face, call him out for the monster that he was and be safe at last.

How it hurt to see Sir Jeffrey taking his ease in one of those brutish masks! But there her husband was, the familiar wave in his greying hair, the breadth of his shoulders, the sturdiness of his shanks, lounging on a divan, waiting for tonight's new girl.

The sink hole eyes glittered. A lecherous moisture slithered in the mouth slit.

He patted his knee. Precedence was established. The new girl was his. He spread his legs and indicated his knee.

Emily went and perched herself...

... Perhaps it would be better to sit properly, beside him, at a little distance first, and engage in polite conversation...

... She balanced on his knee...

... Was she being too forward...?

His hand was already stroking the hot silk rustling on her thigh. He didn't seem to want to talk.

She nestled deeper in his lap, felt the pulsing urgency of his hardening manhood... he who turned away when she came to him in her own body, in her true form!

Surely he'd realize that the moist heat yearning against his stiffening desire was hers! Surely he'd recognize the tang of her desire!

No.

Five years.

It was an eternity since they'd last made love. The succulent yearning squirming against his awakening manhood was a stranger's!

His arm was around her waist already! Too soon! His hand was already straying from her stomach up onto her breasts. Surely he recognized their voluptuous fullness as hers! But no. The red silk ribbons, laced so tight, distorted her breasts into shapes of unimaginable lust.

She put her arms around his neck. She made her best effort to put on a Bethnal Green accent.

"Like a hot notch do you, squire?"

Her sex was certainly hot. It was hotter than it should be, hotter and wetter too.

"Fancy tanning blind cupid, sir?"

Her accent was pathetic—and her husband didn't even recognize her voice!

A grunt.

He liked her hot notch too much to bother with words. He fancied tanning blind cupid too eagerly to waste time speaking.

She sank down onto his penis. She would have liked to kiss but their masks forbade it. He didn't know who she was, or care. And if truth be told, it was so long since they'd lain together her squirming heat no longer recognized the steady pulsing rhythm of his manhood.

Madame chortled.

"She's a hot 'un, Sir..." The bawd was so excited '... *Jeffrey*' tottered on the tip of her tongue. She snatched 'Sir Jeffrey' back just in time and merely said: "... Our Posy likes a good strong whacking steamer!"

Perhaps Madame was right! Perhaps Posy did!

Something dreadful was happening. Her husband's hand was inside her pantaloons. His familiar fingers that held his fork so fastidiously and signed his signature so conscientiously were toying with her clitoris, playing with her helpless wetness, slipping and sliding and sinking into the succulent envelope between her legs.

"... Oh... oh..."

The other men were all watching, jealousy flashing in leather eye holes, their consorts bristling at the speed with which she was arousing him, the speed at which she was getting aroused herself, the immediacy with which she rushed towards the brink. The new girl was showing them up.

"... Yes... yes... yes..."

His fingers exulted in her quagmire's jerking lust. She was too quick. She was climaxing *in front of other people!* Too Fast! Too desperate! She'd told Madame that she was a Bethnal Green dollymop, a Covent Garden regular, not a rejected wife frantic to be fingered!

"... Oh... oh... oh God... yes... ye-eeeeees..."

Her bottom kicked. Her vagina jerked. She rutted on his fingers. Hot humiliation broke over her in waves of burning heat. Something terrible was happening.

"... Yes... yes... ye-eeeeeeeeeeeeeeeeeeeeeeeeeeeeeeeees...!"

She caught fire. Under her bird-of-paradise beak, her face flamed.

At least she was ready now. At least she was fully prepared for accepting her husband's seed. Five minutes alone with him in the bedroom and it would all be over.

He grunted.

A nod.

It was the signal.

He removed his hand from her pantaloons and lifted her off his knee.

He took her hand.

Surely he recognized her fingers. He'd kissed them often enough.

An aroused ape crushed her hand in its imperious grip and led her into a bedroom.

CHAPTER SIX: IN MADAME'S BOUDOIR

Gilt finials. Swags of crimson velvet. A luxurious bed. Straps and ropes around the walls. A contraption of many chains, like a pulley in a cotton mill, hanging from the ceiling.

She struggled in his arms.

"Kiss me! Kiss me, my lord!"

Her lips thrust from under the bird of paradise beak. She wrestled his mask up a few inches and uncovered his mouth. She needed to taste her husband's familiar mouth, the warm generosity of his lips.

He guffawed: "Kiss you, bitch?"

A braying laugh.

"I'll do more than confounded kiss you!"

"Lord...?"

A snarling smile.

A fleshy leer battened on her lips...

... Gross hands pushed the leather snout up higher...

... Shucked the monkey face off entirely...

... Lord Penrose's predatory upper lip, his fleshy snarl, his donkey's bray battened on her helpless cry.

"... Lord...?"

She nearly gave herself away and cried his name out loud.

"I'm not here to bill and coo, you God damned strumpet!"

He threw his mask on the floor.

His face was so imbued with lust he no longer cared who saw. Every God damned strumpet in Hampshire could call his name from the rooftops, so long as he could exact his brute viciousness on her helpless body.

"A filthy little trollop, what?"

"... Yes... no... yes I..."

Big and burly. The same build as her husband. His tie and tails and skin-tight trousers packed with ramping lust.

It was impossible. It couldn't be.

She'd seen her husband hurrying down the alleyway. She'd seen Sir Jeffrey with her own eyes slipping in through the dark door. Her husband was here, but...

... This wasn't he...!

... Her husband was still out in the reception room with a girl on his knee waiting to be beaten...!

Sir Jeffrey Henshawe and Lord Grinley Penrose were of equal rank. They stood shoulder to shoulder in Hampshire society. Both lords of the realm. Both knighted. The dreadful truth came home to her— *they'd both wanted her*, they'd flipped a coin and Lord Grinley had come up trumps.

He was breathing heavily. The dreadful panting of an aroused beast hissed from his distended nostrils.

"Come..."

A dining chair, a single chair from a dining table, stood in the center of the room. It creaked as Lord Penrose settled his weight on it.

"... Come now, Posy..." He leered at her. "... I know you've been a bad girl..." He patted his knee. "... Come and tell your confessor..." *Confessor?* He was an Inquisitor, not a confessor! "... All the bad things you've been doing lately..."

Bend over? Drape her body over his muscular knees? Prostrate herself, bottom up, in his ramping lap?

No. It couldn't be. It was impossible.

She'd rather rip her mask off! Expose her shame! Beard him, face to face! Throw his turpitude back in his confounded eyes! Threaten to tell Lady Penrose!

... But then...

... Admit that she'd offered her body for a whipping in this ghastly place...?

... Confess that she'd pursued Sir Jeffrey to this torture chamber...?

... Face ignominy and penury and still not achieve her goal or conceal the author of her pregnancy...?

Lord Grinley ogled her captive breasts. He patted his knee more firmly.

"Come, Posy. I'm sure you've been a very naughty girl."

A naughty girl?

He could only mean Jonathon! Somehow this brute had found out! Lord Grinley had learned about her and Jonathon swything on the dovecote floor!

He patted his knee.

"Come, Posy. Whisper some delicious sins in your old confessor's ear!"

Delicious sins? There was nothing more delicious than Jonathon's prodigious manhood plowing the succulent spasms of her fertile furrow.

She lay across his knee. She draped her silky stomach over his muscular thighs. Her head hung down. Her hair fell loose and brushed against the floor. Her ankles dangled on the other side, her bottom more naked than it had ever felt in her life.

She waited for the first smack.

Nothing.

Not even the lightest of slaps.

Not even a lecherous tickle.

Rough fingers squeezed her bottom's voluptuous cheeks. A thick fingertip spread her succulent as-crease. It slid down and dallied on her anus.

"Well?"

She didn't understand. He couldn't mean her and Jonathon. She was the only one who knew of that sweet sin.

Lord Penrose thumbed her tailbone. His fingertip slid from her roundmouth to the moister mouth pulsing between her legs.

"I'm waiting, Posy?" *Waiting for what?* "I'm sure you're the wickedest of girls!"

A confession. *He required a confession of her.* Not Jonathon. Something even worse than Jonathon. He thrived on bestial secrets and unspeakable crimes.

She couldn't think of a single thing. She almost confessed to the time she raised her voice to the butler. No. That wouldn't do. She was Posy from Covent Garden with the willing buttocks and savage flashman.

"... I... I... I once... *I once stole a steamer's pocket watch*..."

WHACK!

"Ow!"

The force of the blow juddered her prostrate body. The burning sting jellied her shapely softness. The heat of his palm spread outwards over her quaking bottom.

"That was very naughty of you, Posy!"

WHACK!

"Ouch!"

"And what did you do with that stolen pocket watch?"

"... I...... I... *I sold it!*... I flogged it for three guineas..."

WHACK!

"OW-EEEEEEEEE...!"

The blow came down with dreadful force.

He was a brute. A loathsome beast. His inclinations more vicious than any animal's.

WHACK!

"OW-EEEEEEEEEEEEEEEEEEE...!"

The venom of a lifetime's waking to Lady Penrose's dried-out face percolated through her voluptuous softness.

He panted:

"And? Come! What else?"

Her brain was a blur. She had no idea what crimes a lady of the night might commit.

Blackmail.

"OUCH!"

Snitching.

"OW-WWWWWWW!"

Cheeking a peeler.

"OW-EEEEEEEEEEEEEEEEE!"

Red silk strained at the rim of a luscious volcano. Her bottom turned to a mess of throbbing larva, each blow sinking deeper and deeper, finding the bony resistance in her melting softness, sending wave after wave of awful pleasure thrilling up her body. Lord Grinley Penrose was smacking her bum *and she liked it!*

"More! More! Details! I want more details! You're a cunning little vixen! You're a hot little murderess, aren't you!" *Murderess?* "A lying little body snatcher, ey?" *Body snatcher?* "I'll teach you, you murderous little strumpet! Come on! Tell me! TELL ME!"

WHACK!

"OW-EEEEEEEEEEEEEEEEEEEEE...!"

Her bottom burned beneath his hand.

"... I... I..." She couldn't think. "... I stole my flashman's cigar!..." Worse and worse. She knew a flashman was a gigolo, but she wasn't sure if flashmen smoked cigars. "... I stole my flashman's Havana cigar and smoked it all the way down to the butt..." She wasn't even sure if cigars had a butt or not.

"Oh! You did, did you?"

WHACK!

"OUCH!"

"Right down to the butt, ey?"

WHACK!

"OW!"

She was fortunate. She'd struck upon a good lie. Lord Penrose was thoroughly incensed. The brute was beside himself. He was a man who cherished his cigar.

"Yes, sir. It tasted very fine."

She heard a lucifer strike.

She instantly resented her brazenness.

A sudden acrid smell.

A gust of smoke stung her eyes.

She looked up.

Lord Penrose had a cigar in his mouth! He was returning the card of lucifers to the inside breast pocket of his tail coat. He sucked and puffed with obvious pleasure.

He blew forth a fierce jet of smoke. He chuckled.

"Like a good cigar do you, harlot?"

"... Yes... well... no... well... sometimes..."

She'd been caught out in a lie. Only a white lie. Only a tiny fib but it enraged Lord Grinley beyond all reason.

He reached the cigar down to her mouth.

"Here, Jezebel. Like the best havana, what? HAVE A PUFF!"

Head down, her hair trailing on the floor, her head spun in the giddy fumes.

He shoved the wad of damp cigar-end between her lips. Ugh! The taste of his saliva and sucked tobacco leaf!

The smoke coursed upwards inside the mask, between her golden beak's jeweled cheeks and the helpless steeples of her cheekbones.

Her eyes watered. She coughed and spluttered. She choked on the cigar butt, snatching for air, trying not to breathe.

WHACK!

This smack was so angry it jellied her from head to toe.

WHACK!

WHACK!

WHACK!

He struck her across the bottom again and again. Her whole rear end was on fire, her naked softness a quaking jelly of frantic need.

"... Yes... yes..."

"Lying little slut are you, doxy?"

"... Yes... no..."

WHACK!

His rage wasn't human. He was a crazed animal. He was enraged beast on the jungle floor determined his genes were going to survive.

"Go on, you filthy slut. INHALE!"

She sucked in a lungful of stinging smoke. She choked on the foul stuff. She spluttered on a reeking cloud of smoke. The smoke plundered her throat, thrust a vaporous phallus down past her Adam's apple.

"... I can't... I can't... I won't..."

WHACK!

WHACK!

He wouldn't stop smacking her.

"... Please... please..."

She'd never smoked in her life. Not once. Not even the mildest Virginia, let alone a Havana cigar. Sir Jeffrey made sure to never smoke when he was anywhere in her vicinity.

"... Ple-eeeeeeeeeeeeeease..."

He liked 'please.' Lord Penrose received the word with grim exultation.

"'Please' do you say? Is it 'please ey, Posy'? PLEASE MASTER!"

"Please, master..."

His hot palm kneaded her burning rump. Thick fingers squeezed her sumptuous softness, tested its heat. A fingertip parted her toned, tight crease, dwelt on her quaking tail-bone, slid down her rear crevasse to her ring quaking, its clench of terrible pleasure in a sea of molten pain.

Lord Grinley relieved her of the cigar. He took a few lordly puffs himself and blew hot smoke on the terrible stinging.

"A bum like yours, my dear, it's simply crying out for a good Havana."

He was mad. What was he talking about, 'a good Havana?'

"... Yes... yes..."

Her pleas pleased him. A fingertip slipped into puckered muscle.

"Ow!"

'Ow!' pleased him even more. His fingertip sunk in deeper.

"... Ouch... ow... oh... oh..."

It was unthinkable. She'd never known that such things were possible, that men could sink to such depths of depravity. Women too.

"... Ouch... OUCH... OH GOD...!"

"I'm afraid God's not going to be of much help to you tonight, Posy."

It was unspeakable.

His fingertip was trawling her anal depths. She was a lady. She was the wife of a lord of the land. She'd not been brought up to such things. She'd not been bred to such a travesty.

His finger skewered her rear hole and... *her backside was swiveling on its helpless impalement,* crazed circle after crazed circle of wild excitement enveloping her voluptuous butt.

"... Oh... oh God... yes... yes..."

She felt his finger being replaced...

... *By tobacco leaf...!*

... A thick wad of well-sucked Havana...

... A tight, moist wad of tobacco...

... She knew at once it was the butt end of his cigar...

... Eased into her rear hole...!

"Ow-wwwwwww..."

It wasn't the pain. It wasn't the ghastly slipperiness.

He was humiliating her! Lord Grinley was degrading her. She was the lowest of the low. She was lower than any Covent Garden street walker. He could do whatever he willed with her, whatever monstrous fancy took him. He anchored his monstrous cheroot in her quaking anus, pushed it in, the fierce ember at the far end warming her abused flesh. Thank God it was one of Havana's biggest.

He laughed.

"You smoke better with your pretty little bottom than you do with your mouth, strumpet!"

She rebelled. She would not have it! She was a noblewoman, a lady of the realm! To be subjected to such indignity! But then... if she unfastened her mask... if she showed him her face...her disgrace would be complete... her husband would cast her out... she cried out...

"... 'Twill smoke hotter on your gaying instrument, sir...!"

The foul words sprang too instantly to her lips.

He laughed.

"You say so, Posy?"

Had she longed for this disgrace without once knowing it? Had she dreamed of these indignities in the depths of her nightly oblivion? Had a chaste upbringing and strict code of conduct left her prey to such ghastly intimacies? A surge of lust thrilled through her body. Her rear vice loosened, her molten ring relaxed, sought deeper disgrace. He prigged the cigar in and out of her helpless swiveling.

"... Oh... oh... oh God... yes... *ye-eeeeeees...*"

Pinchcock faking boiled over into heart-felt plea.

"... *Yes... ye-eeeeeeeeeeeeeeeeeeeeees...*"

Her bottom quaked. She rode on his knee, a hundred-weight of helpless longing slumped across a ramping pack-horse.

He growled:

"You're a good little thespian, Posy."

She wasn't a thespian. She wasn't acting at all. She wished she'd stayed at home. She regretted ever coming to this terrible place.

The cigar was halfway consumed before Lord Penrose finally plucked it from her pulsing moue and put it in his mouth.

He rolled the cheroot around between his lips, sucked deep and blew out a jet of hellish smoke.

"Mm-mmmmmmm. Havana never tasted so good!"

She lay panting across his knee. Thank God it was over. At least he'd only tortured her with a cigar. That was something to be thankful for. She'd escaped the whips and paddles hanging from the walls. She'd been spared the rack waiting over in the corner and the pulley hanging from the ceiling.

He squeezed her jellied butt, savored the heat of his night's work. He laughed out loud. Lord Grinley had got his money's worth.

He thrust her roughly from his knee. She fell to the floor.

"Stand up!"

She hurried to her feet.

A mirror mocked her, a masked angel in pantaloons, her crimson buttocks an orangutang's in heat.

Lord Penrose nodded at the hook hanging down from the ceiling. It was a heavy hook suspended on a thick chain, the sort of tackle that hangs from warehouse gantries, meant for lifting heavy weights.

"Up!"

She raised her hands above her head.

"Higher!"

She stretched upwards with both arms.

Lord Grinley produced a pair of leather handcuffs. He shackled her wrists together and attached the cuffs to the hook.

A chain creaked.

There was a tug.

She was lifted onto the balls of her feet.

The chain gnashed its teeth.

Another tug.

"... Oh... oh..."

She was up on tip toes, her toenails scrambling to keep in touch with the floor.

She held her breath and waited for the next tug.

The chain didn't grind a third time. She wasn't jerked up any higher. She wasn't lifted completely off her feet, thank God. Sir Grinley didn't want her to lose consciousness too quickly.

"Sir?"

No answer.

He prowled round and round her. He circled her suspended body, surveyed his prize, his lust so evident he cared nought that his face was fully exposed to a masked prostitute. His eyes were too filled with leering cruelty to care about faces any more.

An arm went round he waist.

"Oh?"

He was an unctuous butcher assessing a dangling carcass, his hand sliding from her hip inside her pantaloons and weighing the heat of the helpless moisture pulsing between her legs.

"A juicy morsel aren't you, Posy?"

"... Yes... yes... I believe I am, sir..."

Rough fingertips found her notch and bathed in love's inlet.

"... Oh... oh..."

She was revolving on her toes like a prima ballerina as he spun her around, the ceiling hook to which she was attached well oiled, relentlessly rotating her.

SMACK!

"Ow!"

A sting like a swarm of bees assailed her buttocks, reminded her what a naughty girl she'd been.

He prowled the room like a ravenous beast studying the range of whips and knouts and paddles hanging from the walls, shopping for the lash that would suit her best.

At other moments they were face to face, her dangling body squashed against his burly weight, his snarling mouth lavishing kisses on her mask, his prigging instrument rock-hard in his pants battering at her pantaloons, a big paw assessing the burning depredations he'd wrought on her baboon's butt.

"Need a good thrashing do you, Posy?"

"... No... yes... I... yes, sir... I do..."

He chose a flail, a hideous cat 'o nine tails she'd seen used on criminals in the stocks.

He draped it over his shoulder and seconded the flail with what could only be a bullwhip.

Round and round he paced, getting himself worked up, at moments stroking the most frightful instrument of all, throbbing in his pants.

He was somewhere behind her.

Emily held her breath.

She couldn't see him any more. She couldn't even hear his tread on the parquet floor. Her face grew hot under her mask. She dared not turn around.

CRACK!

"OUCH!"

He'd seemed so obsessed with her lower parts the sting across her swaddled breasts took her breath away. Cruel leather, tipped with fire, lassoed her shapely softness, caught a nipple in its ferocious clasp.

A ribbon snapped and fell away, released the stinging heat of her succulent fullness.

CRACK!

"OW-WWWWWWW!"

A sizzle between her shoulder blades, a fiery shiver snaking up her spine and the cat's-cradle of ribbons Mary had bound so tight dropped away and her breasts were suddenly completely naked.

He circled her. Round and round her helplessness he stalked, studying, assessing, furling the bullwhip for his next blow, a stockman marshaling a prize heifer at an auction.

A smile at his prowess:

CRACK!

"OW-EEEEEEEEEEEEE...!"

The whip unfurled round her hip. It clasped and stung. Searing leather licked the silky smoothness of her hip bone, bathed her groin in a fiery kiss, snapped the delicate ribbon round her waist. Her pantaloons fell away. Embroidered silk slithered down her knees and puddled on the floor around her toenails.

Lord Grinley jeered:

"A hit! A palpable hit! Venus disrobes, what?"

CRACK!

"... OW-WWWWWWWWWWWWW...!"

He enjoyed whipping dumb beasts. He plied the lash with unparalleled accuracy. He was one of the foremost competitors in the four-in-hand races at Winchester Fair, applying the whip to his mares' rumps with supreme finesse.

He was equally adept with the flail.

CRACK!

"OUCH!"

At moment's the cat 'o nine tails caressed her buttocks, ran tender promises up her quaking softness, paused to forgive her then came down hard and fast, raking her succulent curves with the fires of Hell.

CRACK!

"OW-WWWWWWWWW...!"

He didn't spare her silky flanks. He didn't scruple to torment her voluptuous breasts, to lash her sumptuous fullness, bind her shapely softness in a cat's-cradle of burning welts.

CRACK!

"OW-EEEEEEEEEEEEEEEEE...!"

She danced on tip toes. She went up on one foot. It didn't help. Nothing could lesson the burning hair-shirt Lord Penrose clothed her in.

"OUCH...!...   OUCH...!....   OW! OW-EEEEEEEEEEEEEEEEEEEE...!"

It was too much. It was beyond endurance. She needed to shout out his name, show him she knew who he was, strip off her mask, reveal that he was beating Sir Jeffrey Henshawe's wife, reveal her dreadful secret to the world, be cast out of society and down into the gutter forever.

Impossible. She bit her tongue. She ground her teeth and submitted.

He unzipped his trousers.

"I think that's got you nice and ready, Posy? Ey?"

"... No..."

His gaying instrument swung wildly, long and stiff and mercilessly hard.

"Posy's juicy little slot's hot for some hard prigging, what?"

He tested her wetness. Impossible! It couldn't be! Her notch *was* hot! Love's inlet was moist and melting! Cock alley was yearning to be swythed!

"... Please, sir... no..."

Pleading with him only galled his lust. Her cries were all a pleasurable part of his fiendish game.

He spun her round, suspended on her hook. Round and round. Making her wait. Choosing his moment to plunge his monstrous weapon into her molten place of love.

What if she wasn't pregnant?

The thought hit her like a clap of thunder.

What if Mary was right, and her conviction that she was pregnant just nerves and hysteria?

She shuddered, struck by lightning.

What if she hadn't conceived by Mister Gilbey after all? Their congress on the dovecote floor had been a mere fortnight ago. She had no definite proof that Jonathon had whelped her! What if she was still a heifer, and not a cow, as Lord Grinley would put it? *She might end up having Lord Penrose's child!* His manhood was long and thick and pulsing with a dreadful life force. She'd end up knocked up by this monster! Cast into the gutter and carrying Lord Grinley Penrose's bastard!

He spun her round so she had her back to him. He wasn't interested in her face or its pretty mask.

His big hands closed around her breasts. Strong fingers mauled her tits from behind, fingered the torture he'd inflicted on her toned softness, drew her to him. She felt his throbbing spear-head ease into the laxity his cigar had left behind, his thick tip contemplate the pleasures waiting in her raw rear tunnel—perhaps even hotter and headier pleasures than

the bliss of love's proper inlet— his pulsing spear-head stretch her
roundmouth wide with shock.

"... Ouch... ow... oh... oh..."

He hissed in her ear.

"Like that do you, harlot?"

"... Yes... yes... I like it..."

She did too. His pulsing spear-head plumbed her bottom's burning
vice.

"... Oh... oh..."

Ripples of gratitude run up her body. She spasmed in delicious relief.

"... Ouch... ouch... oh... oh-hhhhhhh...!"

His prodigious engine sank hard and hot and deep into her bottom's
quaking meltdown.

"Like a good buggering, what?"

"... Please... please..."

His ramping steed thumped thrust after thrust into her rear heat. It
hurt, but in her thankfulness and relief he could hurt her as much as he
liked, give her a balsamic injection where and when he chose.

"... Ouch... ow...!... ow-eeeeeeeeeeeee...!"

She saddled herself on his thick cock. She rode his stallion whore
pipe with all the need and desperation inside her. Her roundmouth
jellied on savage insertion after savage insertion, took him harder and
deeper and fiercer than any pinchcock whore had ever taken him before.

"... Yes... yes..."

She was wily. She grew shrewd. She was a witch. She enchanted him
with her back avenue. Her blind cupid mesmerized him. He tupped
her hard and hot. He'd back for some buttered bun *right here* for sure.
Right here and nowhere else. There'd be no sloppy seconds in the sweet
place where children are made. Emily rode him with every ounce of the
passion she had inside her. He could give her as big a balsamic injection
as he liked, as many as he liked, so long as it was *here*.

"... Yes... yes... oh God... yes... ye-eeeeeeeeeeeeeeeeeeeees...!"

She climaxed for him, impaled again and again on his rutting steed. She let the flood of bliss take hold. She gave her body up to the ultimate sting.

"... Yes... yes... ye-eeeeeeeeeeeeeeeeeeeeeeeeeeeees...!"

And she was safe. Lord Grinley Penrose was pumping his lordly semen so hard and hot into her blind cupid there'd be no further attempt on her helplessness.

****

Galloping home in the brougham, in her maid's arms, wrapped in a sheet Mary had snatched off the boudoir bed, Emily wept.

"It's over! I'm finished! Nothing works!"

"There there, my lady. Don't distress yourself."

"I'll never go back there again!"

Her bottom burned. Her rear passage stung execrably, her blind cupid was still raw and sticky from her beating and the overflow of the beast's flood of bliss.

The brougham banged and rattled down darkened country lanes. Emily sobbed uncontrollably. The horror of her situation loomed bigger and darker, more and more evident.

She'd just participated in a bestial act, participated willingly, even vigorously in the sin of Sodom, and she was still no closer to concealing her love for Jonathon, or its proof— if she was indeed pregnant— from her husband.

"Oh God, Mary! What am I going to do?"

It was small comfort that she'd at least avoided being knocked up by Lord Grinley. It was no comfort at all. The thrust and stab of his prodigious engine up her back avenue pursued her in the brougham's every jolt and rattle. She'd escaped recognition, but how would she maintain her composure when Lord Penrose next sat opposite her at the tea table with his bored wife?

The brougham rocked in galloping darkness, a devilish conveyance whisking her off to Hell.

"I'm lost, Mary. It's hopeless!"

Far worse than her physical pain was the knowledge she'd gained about herself.

In little over a week she'd learned the ghastly truth about her own nature.

She'd committed adultery twice. Just eight days ago she'd fornicated with a stranger on the floor of her husband's dovecote. On the strength of a single swything she'd become besotted with a man who cared more about his scientific discoveries than he did about her. Her loyalty to her husband had evaporated in the heat of a single tupping. Even worse than her disloyalty had been her willingness to lie to Sir Jeffrey, her readiness to trick and deceive her husband. She deserved every flinch and sting of the whipping Lord Grinley had given her, every thrust and stab his prodigious engine had speared into her rear tunnel, but worse still—what damned her forever, made her a creature of the deepest-dyed blackness—*she'd enjoyed even that!* Her vicious nature had feasted on the crime of Sodom and on the monstrous way Lord Grinley administered it!

CHAPTER SEVEN: AN ANTIDOTE TO DESPAIR

Sir Jeffrey returned to Henshawe Hall the following morning. He kissed her complacently and went about his business with his usual bland sangfroid.

Studying her husband's face as he stooped to peck her on the cheek it was hard to believe that just twelve hours earlier he'd been hurrying through a darkened doorway into a whipping establishment.

No peck on the cheek could blot out the thought that he'd lounged in Madame's reception room casting a glittering eye through apish eye-holes at the jaded delicacies on display. Emily wondered which of the poor trulls he'd had chosen for his pleasure last night, after Lord Grinley baggsed her, which pair of pantaloons her husband had pulled down, which naked bottom he'd unleashed his criminal desires upon.

Her own crime, however, was greater than his. There was no comfort in dwelling on her husband's vicious desires after the bestial things she'd done with Sir Grinley and the even more treacherous love for Jonathon that burned inside her.

****

The following day she received a second letter from Jonathon. This second epistle was even less satisfactory than the first. There were the same effusions of love and devotion, a few references to 'snatched pleasures' that could have got her into serious trouble if the letter had been intercepted, but the greater proportion of the missive dwelt on his scientific ambitions.

Preparations for the voyage were going well. Mister Darwin was delighted with Jonathon's zeal in getting everything ship shape for the Beagle's second expedition. As well as his nautical preparations, Jonathon was giving well-attended lectures on Natural Selection and participating in the debates on Evolution that had all London talking. He was even writing a book, a companion piece to The Origin of Species, based on his 'happy researches' in Hampshire, regarding which—Emily had the feeling it was the main reason for his writing—he needed some papers that he'd left behind in his hurried exit from Henshawe Hall. Emily would find the papers among some pamphlets and other jottings on a shelf in the 'schoolroom of fondest memory.' He'd be most grateful if she could mail them to him in London post haste.

****

The schoolroom was quiet.

Emily found the required papers easily enough, forty unbound pages covered with Jonathon's brusque, manly handwriting.

'*The Dinosaurs Take Wing.*'

What a curious title!

She needed distracting and *The Dinosaurs Take Wing* was certainly a teasing title.

She pulled a chair up by a sunny window and began to read.

It all began one hundred and forty four million years ago... 144,000,000 *years?*... her head spun.

... A *feathered* dinosaur...

... *A dinosaur with feathers?*...

... Called a theropod began to hunt exclusively in trees...

... The dinosaur shrunk in size for better predatory performance, hopping from branch to branch...

... Evolving can mean shrinking as well as getting larger...?

... *And its forelegs developed into bat-like wings...*

... Page 31 was an engraving of a fossil 'Archaeopteryx', of the same species as Tyrannosaurus Rex and Diplodocus but with... yes!... bat-like wings where its dinosaur forelegs had once been...!

... Over the course of millions of years...

Outside the window feathered tyrannosaurus rexes chirruped in the trees and winged diplodocuses soared into the sky.

By the time she reached the final page, Emily was a convinced Darwinian.

Knowledge! Learning! Understanding! They brought their reviving cordial to her parched lips.

She immediately set about extending and deepening her studies.

She devoured 'The Origin Of Species' cover to cover. She'd only read Jonathon's fly-leaf poem before, now she pored over every single one of Mister Darwin's words.

She delved into volumes by Lamark and Alfred Russell Wallace in Sir Jeffrey's library.

The breadth and grandeur of Mister Darwin's conception thrilled her. Darwin, and Jonathon too, had hit upon a Process more sublime than anything God could ever come up with.

CHAPTER EIGHT: CRISIS

Her period was due.

The day came and went.

Another day.

Three days. Four. Her time of month had always been so regular, but now a week had passed, and still no sign of her menstrual flow.

She was pregnant. She was pregnant by Mister Gilbey with no way to prove otherwise.

"Oh God, Mary! What am I going to do?"

It was the end. She was to be ruined. Just when she'd found a new interest in life, her life was to be destroyed, a poor mutation not strong enough to withstand the slings and arrows of natural selection.

"I'm ruined!"

"Hush, maam. Fretting won't fix nothing."

To return to the establishment in Winchester and make a second attempt on her husband's sadism was beyond her powers. She'd never set foot in Madame's establishment again. Neither did she have the heart to attempt straightforward seduction a second time. She'd tried that and failed miserably. Sir Jeffrey's disinterest in sexual congress with his lawfully wedded wife was as absolute as ever. Nature would take its course and in a month, two of months, at the very most, her adultery would be made evident to the whole world.

Emily paced her bedroom. She plucked at her luxuriant mane.

"What will I do? What ever shall I do?"

"Don't cry, maam. We'll think of something, my lady."

Emily pressed her face to the glass. The park outside blurred with hot tears.

"Think of something? What? *What?* It's hopeless!"

Mary did her best to comfort her. Finally she murmured:

"There's nothing else for it. My lady will just have to use her womanly wiles."

"*Wiles?* What wiles?"

In her frustration Emily almost struck out at Mary.

"Am I to walk into his bedroom in pantaloons and a mask? Hand him his bull-whip? Cock blind cupid? *He'll abhor me!*"

"Nothing so brazen my lady, but..." Mary grinned. "... Did my lady learn nothing in Madame's establishment?"

Learn? What was the stupid girl talking about, 'learning'?

"Experience, maam... even of the most ghastly type... is always educational."

Her maid was lecturing her! Emily studied the young woman's face.

"Are you serious?"

"Serious as I can be, maam."

"And you think it'll work?"

"You have no other option."

****

Emily waited till the following Friday.

Friday was her husband's day for traveling to Winchester.

She waited till the hours immediately before his departure. The frisson of excitement he was no doubt experiencing, readying himself for his trip to Madame's, might be of some aid in her stratagem.

She found Sir Jeffrey in his study, sitting at his desk packing up some parliamentary papers into the attache case he always took with him to Winchester.

"My lady!"

His mouth fell open. His eyes went wide with shock.

She was barefoot, her hair disheveled, her face deathly pale.

"... Forgive me, Sir Jeffrey... I beg your forgiveness!"

"Forgiveness?"

He stared at the flimsy cotton shift which was all that she was wearing.

"...Yes.... Forgive me... I'm a bad girl..."

"Girl?"

Thirty years old? She was hardly a girl, yet suddenly her heart was racing like an eighteen-year-old's.

"... I... I..."

She flung herself across his knee.

Lord Grinley had demanded a confession. Lord Penrose had needed to hear Posy recite her sins in order to prime his lust. He'd called himself her 'old confessor.'

"... I... I've done something wicked... very very wicked..."

Her wickedness was without bounds but confessing her real crimes now was out of the question.

Sir Jeffrey chuckled.

"Wicked? I'm sure my good wife is not capable of a deed deserving such a dreadful word."

She squirmed, face down across his knees. He tried to remove her from his lap but she pulled her shift up higher.

"... I am... I swear it... I'm beyond the pale..."

His fingers fidgeted with the papers on his desk. The welts she'd received from her thrashing at Lord Penrose's hands had healed. The last traces of her beating had vanished away. Her naked bottom was as toned and voluptuously rounded as it had ever been. He didn't want to touch it.

"Come now, darling." He laughed. "'Tis just a fit of the vapours. A moment's hysterics. Beyond the pale?"

His knees squirmed awkwardly beneath her, trying to get her naked buttocks out of his lap.

"... Yes... yes... I'm a bad girl... *I released your prize pigeon...!*"

"*You what?*"

"... Methuselah... your prize racer... I released him from his cage..."

A baffled roar.

"*EY?*"

"... While Tommy was training the falcon... and the falcon swooped and..."

"IT WHAT?!!"

"... The falcon mangled Methuselah, sir, and... and..."

"AND?!!!!"

WHACK!

"OW!"

His hand came down hard and hot on her naked bottom. His broad palm stung the shapely softness of her derriere. There was no holding back. The blow was delivered with the full force of all his anger.

WHACK!

"OUCH!"

Her blind cupid stung. Love's rear orbs jellied under the fury of his blows.

"Methuselah?"

"... Yes... yes... I'm a bad girl... hit me... hit me harder...!"

He obeyed. The blows rained down like claps of thunder on her quaking softness.

"... OUCH... OW... OH... OH... OW... OW-EEEEEEE...!"

Somewhere beneath her, where her naked belly rode the fury of his thighs a gathering hardness ticked against her stomach. Sir Jeffrey was more than angry.

"... You bitch... confounded jade..."

"... Yes... yes... beat me... beat me harder... whip me... give me my just deserts...!"

"Your just deserts? I'll give you your just deserts, strumpet!"

He dragged her out of his lap. He threw her face down on the bed, her bottom a burning beacon signaling frantically to his rampant lust.

He snapped the catches of his attache case open and drew out a flail from underneath his papers, a cat 'o nine tails crueler even than Lord Grinley's knout, the thin leather straps viciously knotted.

"How dare you, madam?"

"... Whip me, my lord... teach your strumpet a lesson..."

SLASH!

"... OW...!"

SLASH!

"... OW... OW-EEEEEEE...!"

The blows rained down like a hailstorm of fire on her quaking rump. Her husband applied the whip even harder than Lord Grinley.

"... OUCH... OU-UUUUUUUCH...!"

She parted her thighs, she let him see the succulent moisture awakening between her legs, the molten longing his blows were slamming into her. Her wet heat made him even angrier.

"Filthy jade! Pinchcock whore!

SLASH!

"... OW... OW-EEEEEEEEEEEEEE...!"

She rolled onto her back.

"... Harder, my lord... please punish your bad girl harder..."

He obeyed. He had no alternative. Her toned breasts suffered the whip's burning kisses.

"... OUCH... *OUCH*...!"

Her silky flanks lifted to the burning tendrils of the lash.

"... Whip me harder, my love... OW...!... your strokes are far too kind..."

She made the perilous attempt. She reached out where he reared above her and stroked the merciless hardness pulsing under his tight dress trousers, ran frantic fingernails up his anger's tall relentless prong, thumbed desperately at furious buttons and released his prigging instrument from its formal confinement.

"... Punish your wicked slave..." Yes. 'Slave.' That was the word Lord Penrose had used. 'Slave' was perfect for her. "... Punish your poor slave with your Rod of Wrath...!"

She pumped it with hot fingers. She enfolded it in a fervid palm. She ramped his prodigious instrument. She'd forgotten how big he was. Over five lonely years her memory had let slip the noble dimensions of her husband's manhood. She massaged his pulsing spear-head with slippery fingertips.

"Confounded slut!"

"... Yes... yes..."

A slick of hot semen, the glistening precursor of his largesse and of her salvation, ached on his pulsing tip.

"Wretched strumpet!"

She spread her legs. Her succulent surrender lifted towards where the stroke would fall.

"... Yes... yes... punish your wretched strumpet...!"

"Pinchcock bunter!"

"... Please... please..."

Jove's lightning bolt descended. He unleashed his terrible thunder. His lightning struck where she needed him most, pierced her and kept on going, thundered into her helpless surrender, her lord and master's ramping manhood possessed her succulent depths.

"... Yes... yes... oh God... yes... ye-eeeeeeeees...!"

She rutted on his slamming delivery, rode on her husband's ramping prong, an innocent wife going over the brink again and again on her master's pounding need of her.

"... Oh... oh..."

"God damned..."

The bolt of lightning split her, pumped throb after throb of molten life force into her sopping depths, drenched her deepest and most secret places, filled her ramping tightness and overflowed down her pert bottom, enough luxurious seed to father a thousand generations of Henshawes.

****

He lay on top of her, his engorged prong still pulsing sweet messages into her brimming depths long after the tempest of his delivery was over.

His shoulders heaved.

His body shook.

"... Oh God, Emily..."

She put her arms around him.

He was sobbing. Her husband was weeping on her breast!

She smoothed the muscles quaking on his shoulders. Sir Jeffrey was sobbing inconsolably.

"... It's alright... it's alright..."

"... I'm so so sorry..."

"Sorry, my lord?"

"... I'm a cad... a... a worthless bounder..."

She kissed his ear.

"Ssh-hhhhhh. Don't say so, Sir Jeffrey."

"... I'm a fiend... a monster... I hurt you...!"

"The hurt's already healed, husband."

She meant it. What she said was true. Five years of neglect and disregard were melting away in the sweet intimacy of his big heavy body pressing down on her lithe, voluptuous one.

She kissed his hair. His cheek. His blubbered lips. She had tears in her eyes herself, tears of joy and relief and a sudden reawakening of long buried feelings.

He groaned:

"... Can you ever forgive me...?"

"You're forgiven already, Jeffrey. In fact..."

It was time to tell him about Jonathon. She needed to confess her adultery while this magic moment lasted. It was her chance to admit that she was already pregnant but that carrying another man's child didn't stop her from loving her rightful mate.

She bit her tongue.

"... I... I... took the whip... *to my beloved wife*...!"

"There there. 'Tis nothing."

"Nothing?" It was the howl of pain of a soul writhing on the burning lake. "... You don't understand... I'm a vicious brute..."

He lifted himself on one elbow and stared aghast at the uppermost of her wounds, a lasso shaped welt circling her shoulder where the bullwhip had taken its pleasure on her silky skin.

She whispered:

"Fie! 'Tis nothing! A mere tickle, my lord."

It was time to tell him about her night in Madame's establishment. She needed to confess at least that. This new love felt so good not even the details of Lord Penrose's penetration of her anus could dispel it. And if she told him about her night in the House of the Divine Marquis, he would have to admit his own sins in that establishment. The truth would draw them even closer together. Was that not what the Gospels taught? Mutual forgiveness of sins in this blessed closeness.

He smiled:

"A mere tickle?"

His lips traced the curvature of the welt, kissed away the pain, grazed the sting with a tender buss all the way down her breast, a kiss as light as a butterfly unfolding its moist wings on her shapely softness, a succulent grazing breathing where the whip had bit in, his tongue begging forgiveness of her throbbing nipple.

"... Mm-mmm... a tickle, my lord..."

She offered him her other breast, the inflamed places where he'd scored her sumptuous fullness. His tongue worshiped her toned softness,

"... Yes... yes..."

He kissed the red marks in her cleavage, followed the abrasions down a silky pulse to where her belly, so brutally cross-hatched, rose to grant his lips forgiveness.

"... Oh... oh... oh God... yes...yes... "

Her bottom had taken the worst of his fury. She rolled onto her belly and offered his mouth the burning places where his rage had bitten worst. He nuzzled her taut ass-crease. He tongued her anus. His lips found the maps of stinging heat he'd lambasted into her curvaceous tenderness, his lips followed the lash's burning progress down between her legs.

Had he whipped her even there?

"... Oh... oh... oh God... yes... yes..."

He feasted on her sumptuous wetness. He tongued the wet depths of her succulent surrender. Powerful teeth took hold of her clit, gnawed with infinite gentleness the crazed nub of her deepest desire. He drew his mouth away:

"I love you, my lady."

"... Yes... please... ple-eeeeeeeeease..."

It was too late for confessions. They were beyond guilt and forgiveness. She was already pulsing in helpless climax as his throbbing manhood sank into her again, as his rock-hard need impaled her again and again, waking ecstatic secrets too deep for words.

****

It was late when Emily and her husband came down to dinner, too late for Sir Jeffrey to make his usual trip to Winchester.

CHAPTER NINE: IDYLL

The following months were a blessed idyll, a thriving holiday after the rigors of Madame's establishment and the fraught moment when she'd seduced her husband.

Carrying burdensome secrets wasn't easy but with the announcement of her pregnancy thrilling polite society and Sir Jeffrey's manifest delight and pride it was impossible not to relax and accept the monstrous good fortune of her adultery remaining undiscovered.

Everyone remarked how well motherhood suited her. Emily's eyes took on an added sparkle. Her cheeks found a deeper glow. The growing roundness of her belly only seemed to emphasize how voluptuously well-built she was.

Why should she not enjoy this vacation from care? Jonathon's letters grew more solicitous, conscious of his role as a father.

And Sir Jeffrey?

Her husband was a delight. She'd always known Sir Jeffrey to be a good, honest and noble man, but with the renewal of their sexual relationship goodness and honesty and nobility were imbued with a passionate liking.

His Friday night trips into Winchester were a thing of the past. Yes, her husband needed to whip her to reach the pinnacle of desire, but as the months progressed he wielded the lash so subtly and so intimately their mutual desire reached consummation on deeper and deeper levels, delight at an ever higher pitch.

Autumn came, and then the first frosts of winter. A trip to London was the done thing. Stretched out on the bed in Jonathon's inn Emily found that her love for Jonathon too had only grown stronger, as his love for her had only grown stronger too, and they reached a renewed ecstasy, tasted more and more delicious love cries above the clattering cobblestones and street vendor cries of Whitechapel.

Cuddling together after they'd finished fucking, Jonathon touched her belly with an awed tenderness. It was lovely to lie on her back with her legs voluptuously spread and his generous seed trickling down her bottom onto the sheets, her stomach jutting a little like a hill in paradise. His awed tenderness hardened into a relentless insistence

She rolled over and went up on all fours, her belly swaying. His prigging instrument was still erect. It was months since he'd last seen her and his desire still wasn't sated. Perhaps he fancied taking her from behind?

"What's this?"

"... Oh... oh nothing..."

Sir Jeffrey whipped her so solicitously these days there was little more than an added flush of redness and the faintest cat's-cradle of ghostly lesions.

"... A man of science and you haven't heard of scarifying...?"

"Scarifying?"

"... Scarifying one's skin for extra softness... Mary performs the operation for me..."

She felt his prigging instrument gently graze her renewed softness, his throbbing spear-head register her grateful wetness. The two-backed beast reclaimed its face, her eyes drowning in swan's down, her succulent cupid's-bow wetting the pillow with kisses as this lovely man took her from behind.

****

Emily's avid reading and protracted studies had yielded a rich harvest. She knew more about random mutation and natural selection and hereditary traits and those mysterious things called genes than any woman in Hampshire, and most of the men too.

Her studies in the Theory of Evolution never once abated throughout her pregnancy, her delving into the mysteries of the prehistoric eons only gathered pace after that sunny afternoon in the schoolroom reading about how the dinosaurs took flight.

She gave talks on Mister Darwin's Theory in the village hall and in the reading room of the Winchester Academy of Science. By the fourth month of her pregnancy Emily was famous all around the county as 'that Evolution Lady of Henshawe Hall.'

Sir Jeffrey smiled upon her academic success. He was proud of his learned wife, and when Mister Darwin himself invited Emily up to London to deliver a lecture on Mesozoic Fossils at the Royal Geographical Society her husband was only too pleased to let her 'spread her wings in the Empyrean of Scientific Truth.'

In London Emily dined with Mister Darwin himself. The 'devil' who'd wrecked religion proved to be an amiable old gentleman of sixty, pleased to receive the support of an aristocratic and beautiful young woman of 'capacious intellect.' In fact it was Mister Darwin himself who suggested that Emily accompany he and Mister Gilbey on the forthcoming voyage to the Galapagos Islands. The great man of science was sure that such a refined and educated woman as Lady Emily would 'find much to divert and instruct her' on their journey 'around the Horn.'

This, of course, was impossible. She'd almost come to term. The time to deliver her baby was fast approaching. In fact, with such precise knowledge of the date of conception, the date for her lying in coincided with the spring neap tides and the Beagle's proposed departure.

There was also the minor consideration, which had grown to become a major consideration, that she was in love with two men.

Time closed in. Jonathon was due to embark on the first of March. She'd managed to get the Henshawe Hall physician to prepare Sir Jeffrey for a possible 'premature' delivery to account for the month between the dovecote floor and her husband first whipping her. Now, with her time so close, her joining the expedition was out of the question. Darwin's first expedition had taken a full five years. It was a long time. Rounding the Horn was always a dangerous business, not to mention the savages of Tierra del Fuego and the crazed cultists of Chile and Peru. *She might never see Jonathon again.*

On the other hand, she had a noble and passionate husband, not just a good man but a prodigious stallion into the bargain, so powerfully tender in his love making she could almost say she'd found herself a new species of husband.

The first of March arrived and, right on time, Emily was brought to bed. She cried out. She groaned. She wept. She gnashed her teeth. In the frenzied hallucinations of labour she saw the Beagle striking out from Plymouth Sound, Jonathon on the forecastle, his eyes set on the Southern Atlantic and further discoveries to be made towards the great Idea of Evolution.

But then, there beside her at her bed of pain stood Sir Jeffrey, his eyes shining with manifest love. He didn't hide away like most men did. He was holding her hand as the crisis came.

The baby boy was perfect in every way.

They agreed to name him Charles, in honour of the great theoretician.

Her husband's delight in the child was so sincere, Emily felt only the slightest stab of guilt at his ignorance. She'd make it up to him in every possible way. She thanked God that she'd been spared having to make an impossible choice.

Next day news came from Plymouth.

A storm along the South Coast and forecasts of treacherous tides south of Biscay had delayed the Beagle from weighing anchor. Jonathon's departure had been postponed for a further fortnight.

She hadn't been spared an impossible choice at all.

THE END

BOOK ONE OF *THE STEAMY TRIALS OF A VICTORIAN LADY: IN HIS LORDSHIP'S DOVECOTE*

It's 1868. Darwin's 'Origin of Species', with its message of survival of the fittest and 'nature red in tooth and claw' has shaken the established order. Sequestered in rural Hampshire, Lady Emily Henshawe's problems are closer to home, a childless marriage and a husband who's more interested in breeding pigeons than he is in her. With her thirtieth birthday approaching it's time for Emily to resign herself to a humdrum future, until, that is, Jonathon Gilbey, a young, firebrand follower of Darwin, arrives at Henshawe Hall to conduct experiments on her husband's pigeons. Emily's appalled—that a youth of Jonathon's noble aspect and fine physique should believe in beast eat beast!— and she sets out to save the young man from his atheistic ideas. Love, however, works in mysterious ways and before Emily knows it Jonathon is conducting experiments on her heart, and on her newly awakened body too.

BOOK THREE: *IN HIS LORDSHIP'S DUNGEON*

Lady Emily joins Darwin's second expedition to the Galapagos Islands and falls foul of barbaric cultists.

BOOK FOUR: *IN HIS LORDSHIP'S STUDY*

Lady Emily seeks consolation in religion, but why does God make his clergymen so irresistible?.

Also by Catherine Moorland

Demon Lover Romance
Riding a Monster Wave at BDSM Beach

Steamy Trials of a Victorian Lady
In His Lordship's Dovecote
In His Lordship's House of Ill Fame

Milton Keynes UK
Ingram Content Group UK Ltd.
UKHW010728241123
433194UK00001B/153

9 798223 462583